FOR GAANG

www.fsgkidsbooks.com

Library of Congress Cataloging-in-Publication Data
Yum, Hyewon.
     Last night / Hyewon Yum.— 1st ed.
        p.   cm.
     Summary: Sent to her room for refusing to eat her dinner, a
little girl soon falls asleep and together with her bear friend
begins a fantastic voyage deep into the forest where they dance
and play all night.
     ISBN-13: 978-0-374-34358-3
     ISBN-10: 0-374-34358-6
     [1. Stories without words.   2. Dreams—Fiction.   3. Toys—Fiction.]
I. Title.

PZ7.Y81654 Las 2008
[E]—dc22
                                                    2007030386

Hyewon Yum

LAST
NIGHT

FRANCES FOSTER BOOKS FARRAR STRAUS GIROUX NEW YORK

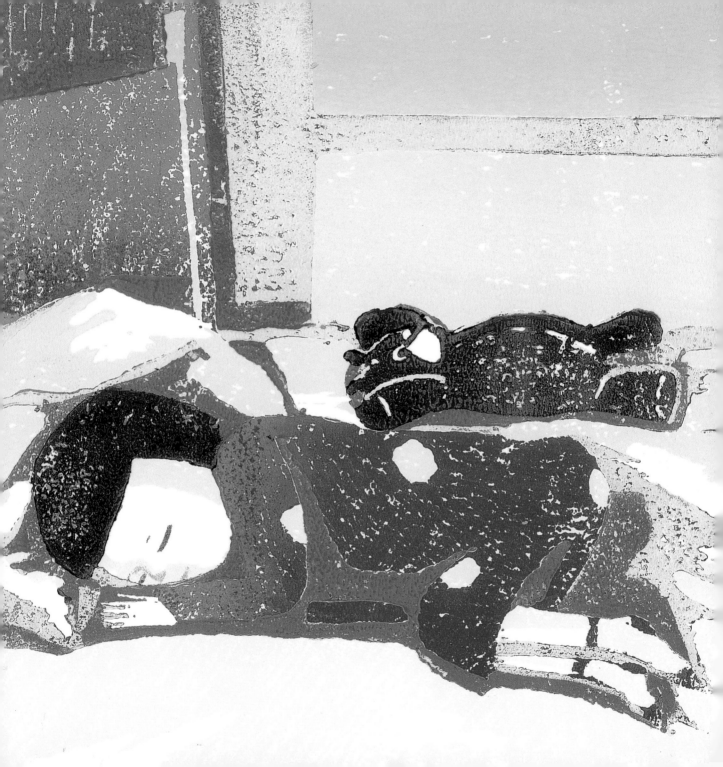